NGOZI UKAZU

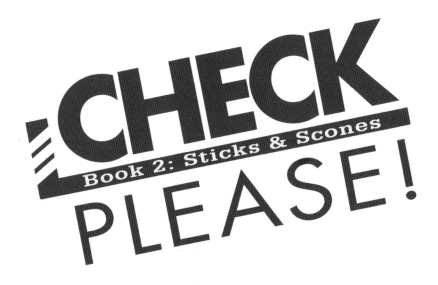

CHECK

Book 2: Sticks & Scones

PLEASE!

:01

First Second

New York

FOREWORD

ERIC BITTLE STARTED OFF as a ballpoint pen sketch in a college-ruled, spiral-bound notebook—a character in the margins with a speech bubble, a hockey jersey, and a pie. Five years, several chapters, and a slew of online comic updates later, he's as far from the margins as he'll ever be. He's the main character of the first graphic novel series I've ever written, and a person with a story.

If the first *Check, Please!* installment, *#Hockey*, was about Bitty discovering himself, then this book, *Sticks & Scones*, is about Bitty announcing himself. It's Eric Bittle reaching his full potential. It's about risk. It's about learning not to be afraid. And it's about realizing you were strong the whole time. We're a very long way away from the idea of "what if a figure skater (and baker!) joined a bro-y NCAA men's hockey team?" We're in Providence, Rhode Island, and Boston, Massachusetts, and Madison, Georgia; we're at center ice in a hockey stadium; and we're following Bitty to the end of Samwell, and into adulthood. We're a very long way from the margins.

This is the second and final *Check, Please!* book and I'm excited to share the end of this series. I will miss Samwell dearly. Just as Bitty discovered who he was in the Haus and in Faber and as a member of the Samwell men's ice hockey team, I learned so much about myself in the pages of this comic. I hope you discover a bit of yourself as well.

P.S. Oh, and please be sure to check out Bitty's tweets in the back of the book. B. "Shitty" Knight does in fact have a first name, and Bitty finally finds out what it is. (And so do we!)

JUNIOR YEAR

WAG

OH, I WON'T MENTION HOCKEY. HECK, I WON'T EVEN MENTION *SAMWELL*.

HAH! YES!!

"HEY, Y'ALL! HE PLAYS A SPORT THAT INVOLVES ICE? YOU GUESSED IT: MY BOYFRIEND'S A COMPETITIVE CURLER."

...I'M SURE YOU'RE WONDERFUL AT CURLING.

THE BOYS? *SHOOT*...I DON'T EVEN THINK THEY KNOW I'M DATING.

THEY'RE STILL TRICKLING IN...ALMOST A FULL HAUS!

OH! AND DO YOU HAVE ANY IDEA WHERE THE KEY TO THE BASEMENT IS? I CALLED SHITTY AND HE HAS NO... UH-HUH.

OKAY... OKAY.

ALL RIGHT! YOU CALL ME RIGHT BACK IF YOU REMEMBER WHERE IT IS.

MMMHM, I'LL COOK 'EM ALL A LIL SOMETHING... I KNOW.

BYE, SWEETHÉART.

2

TADDY TOUR

MEET THE FALCONERS

HOME OPENER

5

THE AFTER KEGSTER

26

HOLY HELL, EXACTLY. YIKES.

YEAH...I GUESS SHITTY WAS COMING FOR HIM LIKE...I DUNNO, LIKE JACK HAD SOMETHING TO HIDE AND I'M LIKE—

RIGHT, *NO*. GUY HAS A *LOT* OF THINGS HE KEEPS TO HIMSELF, BUT IT'S NEVER BEEN THE CHICKS HE'S WHEELING.

Hey, can we skype tomorrow night? I'm getting back late and need to get up early for the roadie. I want to talk to you about the kegster. I'm sorry.

HEY, WELL. BRO JUST HAS *SUPER* LASER FOCUS. WHEN YOU'RE GOING HUNDY-TEN PERCENT ON HOCKEY, NOT ROOM FOR MUCH ELSE, YOU KNOW?

YEAH...

WELL. GLAD HE MADE IT TO THE KEGSTER.

I MEAN, IT'S WHY HE'S FUCKING *INCREDIBLE*.

TOTALLY!

6

PB&J

LVA @ PVD — I

...HM.

YOU TOLD ME WHAT HAPPENED WITH CAMILLA AND THOSE OTHER GIRLS...

HOW'D IT END WITH KENT PARSON?

WELL...HE GOT DRAFTED. I DIDN'T. AND IT...STOPPED. LOOKING BACK, IT REALLY WASN'T ANYTHING MORE THAN PHYSICAL. HOCKEY.

AND AFTER TAKING MY BREAK, THEN SAMWELL... IT TAKES A LOT OF GROWING UP TO REALIZE SOMEONE WASN'T GOOD FOR YOU.

RIGHT. YOU HAVE TO THINK ABOUT YOUR CAREER.

AND IT KIND OF HAD AN EXPIRATION DATE FROM THE GET-GO, YOU KNOW?

PUSH COMES TO SHOVE... HOCKEY CAME FIRST.

SOMETHING LIKE THAT COULD'VE REALLY MESSED WITH OUR CAREERS.

JACK, HOW ARE YOU PREPARING FOR THE ACES NEXT WEEK?

THIS IS YOUR FIRST ENCOUNTER IN A RINK SINCE YOU WON THE MEMORIAL CUP TOGETHER...

THERE'S A LOT OF HISTORY, ISN'T THERE?

BUT YOU AND KENT PARSON—

AH, JUST, YOU KNOW— STICKING TO OUR GAME. WE'VE BEEN ON A GOOD RUN AT HOME.

YEAH.

BUT IT'S ALL IN THE PAST.

LVA @ PVD — II

HI, HONEY — I

BUT YOU TOLD ME TO CALL IF I EVER... NEEDED YOU.

AND I NEEDED TO GET THIS OUT NOW.

I GUESS...MAYBE *HIDING* THIS HAS BEEN HARD LATELY.

AND I KNOW THE BOYS ARE STARTING TO THINK SOMETHING'S UP.

YAWN!

EVERYONE'S BEEN GIVING IT 100% AT PRACTICE, BUT I KNOW I HAVEN'T.

HI, HONEY — II

11

ME & JACK

BITTY & I

TELLING MY PARENTS ABOUT US?

YOU'D WANT THAT?

NO...HONEY. THAT'S...THAT WOULD MEAN A LOT TO ME.

LET'S TALK ABOUT IT.

OF COURSE. MY DAD WOULD HAVE GOOD ADVICE AND...MY MOM HAS BEEN ASKING ABOUT YOU A LOT ANYWAY.

I WANT THEM TO KNOW ABOUT YOU. I UNDERSTAND IF THAT'S—

RIVERSIDE

HOCKEY-WISE? OUR FRIEND JACK— SAMWELL'S FORMER CAPTAIN AND STARTER FOR THE NHL'S PROVIDENCE FALCONERS—

IT'S RARE— SURE—

—WAS HONORED WITH THE ROLE OF ALTERNATE CAPTAIN FOR HIS IMPACT AND LEADERSHIP ON THE TEAM!

—BUT RARELY HAS ANY PLAYER CONTRIBUTED SO MUCH TO THE SUCCESS AND LEADERSHIP OF A TEAM SO QUICKLY.

(Y'ALL, THE FALCS' *LEADING SCORER!*)

ALL OF US AT SAMWELL ARE SO PROUD OF THIS BOY.

⸮SIGH⸮ *I'M* SO PROUD OF HIM!

ALTHOUGH SAMWELL IS FAR FROM FIRST IN THE STANDINGS—

HM. MAYBE IT'S EASIER TO GIVE 100% WHEN YOU CAN BE 100% YOURSELF!

OH, SHE DID IT.

SHE *REALLY* DID IT.

—WE'VE ALL BEEN PLAYING HOCKEY TO BE PROUD OF.

I KNOW I'VE FELT GOOD ON THE ICE AS OF LATE, TOO.

WHAT?

OH, WOW, HAHA.

THANKS, SUZANNE.

69

SHE'S BEEN TALKING ABOUT BUYING YOUR JERSEY **FOR MONTHS** AND NOW THAT YOU'VE GOT THE "A"— MY MAMA AND COACH ARE SO PROUD. AND SHE WATCHED THE JERSEY CEREMONY? LET ME TELL YOU, SHE'S GOT THE **BIGGEST CRUSH** ON MARTY AND THIRDY.

I'M CRAZY 'CAUSE I WATCHED ALL THE **FACEOFFS**, BUT **SHE'S** WATCHED ALL THE ONES THAT THIRDY AND MARTY ARE IN AND SHE KEPT GOING ON AND ON!

SOME OF THE FALCS? HONEY, THEORETICALLY, I'D LOVE TO, BUT—

HAHA, REALLY?

"DICKY, I'M MARRIED BUT I'M NOT DEAD!! HAVE YOU MET THEM? YOU SHOULD TRY TO MEET 'EM!!"

HAH, WELL...

LIKE WE ALL COULD SET UP A COFFEE DATE FOR WEDNESDAY! GOOD LORD.

...WOULD YOU EVER WANT TO MEET THEM? SOME OF THE GUYS?

HEY.

HUH?

LET'S TAKE THE LONG WAY BACK TO CAMPUS, EH?

MONDAY IN THE PARK
WITH GEORGE

I CAN **STILL** CALL THIS A BAKING VLOG SINCE THE RELATIONSHIP QUESTIONS HAVEN'T OUTNUMBERED THE RECIPES.

THE PERSONAL STORIES HAVEN'T OUTPACED THE PIE? (MORE LOAF TALK THAN LOVE TALK?)

BUT THAT IS A GOOD QUESTION.

HM. THE THING IS... IT'S DIFFERENT FOR EVERYONE. AND IT'S DIFFERENT EVERY TIME.

TELLING PEOPLE ABOUT WHO YOU'RE DATING OR WHO YOU ARE—IT'S NOT A **ONE-AND-DONE** TYPE OF THING!

IT'S SOMETHING YOU'LL LIKELY HAVE TO DO OVER AND OVER (AND OVER AND OVER).

15

DINNER AT MARTY'S?

HELP WANTED

REALLY, RANSOM?!

ADAM BIRKHOLTZ, WHY ON **EARTH** ARE YOU SHOUTING AT RANSOM IN COMMONS AT 7 AM?

I— SORRY.

DUDE! BACK **THE FUCK** OFF! I'VE BEEN DOING THE INTERVIEWS SINCE NOVEMBER AS A **PLAN B.** YOU KNEW—

BUT I DIDN'T KNOW YOU WERE **SERIOUS— SERIOUS** ABOUT CONSULTING.

IT'S SELFISH, SOULLESS, CORPORATE, LIBERAL ARTS GRAD **GRUNT WORK.**

HOLSTER...YOU WANT TO GO INTO CONSULTING!

I'M AN ECON MAJOR, CHRISTOPHER!

YOU'RE GIVING UP ON BIO!

YOU **LIKE** BIO. AND DOCTOR STUFF.

I KNOW, I'M, LIKE, MAJORING IN BIO AND DID PRE-MED...

AND HELPING PEOPLE AND STUFF IS IMPORTANT OR WHATEVER.

BUT MY *PARENTS* WANT ME TO BE A DOCTOR. MY SISTER'S A PHARMACIST AND MY OTHER ONE WANTS TO DO ENGINEERING.

WE'D BE THIS WEIRD TRIFECTA OF *NIGERIAN PARENT EXPECTATIONS*.

BUT...YOU AND SHITTY ARE LIKE THE SMARTEST BROS I KNOW.

DON'T YOU WANNA BE LIKE HIM? MAKE THE WORLD A BETTER PLACE WITH YOUR BRAIN?

IDK. I KINDA WANT TO MAKE MONEY?

SAME.

SOFT SAME.

LARDO! WHAT ARE YOU GONNA DO AFTER YOU GRAD—

I. DON'T. KNOW. YET.

OH, HAHA 'SWAWESOME!

LARDO, UM, HAS BEEN A *TAD* STRESSED BECAUSE WE'RE TRYING TO FIND A NEW MANAGER. BUT WE'RE ALL PITCHING IN TO HELP!

87

DIB FLIP

YEAH, BUT YOU CAN LIVE **ANYWHERE** ON CAMPUS—GETTING OFF THE MEAL PLAN AND PAYING HAUS RENT ACTUALLY SAVES ME—

HEY, BITS.

WHAT ON **EARTH** ARE THEY BICKERING ABOUT?

OH MY **GO-O-OD!** POINDEXTER! YOU'RE NOT THE ONLY GUY AT SAMWELL PAYING ROOM AND BOARD—

BITTY, **PLEASE** REASON WITH—**AGHH!!!**

BITTY, DEX IS BEING —**OOF.**

STOP IT.

UGH!

THEY'RE ARGUING ABOUT **MY DIBS.**

YOUR **DIBS?** I THOUGHT YOU WERE GIVING THEM TO OLLIE? OR—ER—WAS THAT WICKY?

I WAS—

BUT RANS AND HOLSTER HAD THEM **BOTH** LOCKED DOWN FOR THE ATTIC BACK IN FEBRUARY AND NEVER TOLD ME.

'SWAWESOME

THESE TWO *DUMMIES* FOUND OUT FROM OLLIE THIS MORNING. AND IF THEY DON'T SHUT UP I'M GIVING MY ROOM TO *TANGO.*

IT'S NOT THAT YOU DON'T DESERVE DIBS, DEX—BUT I WAS BANKING ON YOU GETTING THE AT—

YOU WERE *BANKING*?!

ENOUGH. FULL TEAM LOTTERY. ONLY FAIR.

SORRY, BUT *HOW* DOES NURSEY DESERVE DIBS?

DEX. I KNOW YOU FIXED A TON OF STUFF IN THE HAUS THIS YEAR. BUT NURSEY PROOFREAD EVERY ART CRITICISM RESPONSE I TURNED IN THIS SEMESTER.

HE PRACTICALLY WROTE MY SENIOR THESIS.

AND HE GETS A WEIRD KICK OUT OF FIXING BIBLIOGRAPHIES.

THAT LAST PART'S FAKE.

LADY AND GENTLEMEN.

THIS MIGHT NECESSITATE A *DIB FLIP.*

OH SHIT. GOOD THINKING, BITTY!

I MEAN, IT'S WHAT THE BYLAWS ARE *FOR!*

IN LIEU OF A LOTTERY, A COIN FLIP CAN DECIDE THE TRANSFER OF DIBS BETWEEN MULTIPLE PARTIES.

NOW, IF YOU TWO SHAKE HANDS WE CAN GET THIS OVER WITH. *FAIR AND SQUARE.*

ONE FLIP.

WILL? DEREK?

HUH. POINDEXTER.

NURSE.

'SWAWESOME.

FAMILY SKATE

HEY, Y'ALL!! IF I SEEM A LITTLE JITTERY IT'S BECAUSE TONIGHT? I'M MEETING A BUNCH OF MY BOYFRIEND'S COWORKERS.

AND THEY'RE ALL NICE AND WONDERFUL, AND HE'S TALKED ABOUT ME BEFORE. *BUT...*

UH. SO THIS NEXT VIDEO IS GONNA BE ON CHOOSING A FOUR-PIE COMBO THAT WILL WIN STRANGERS OVER AND MAKE THEM NOT HATE YOU!

19

KEAGSTER

HEY, Y'ALL...
≶SIGH≷

SO. OUR SEASON IS OVER.

SOMETIMES THEY END WITH A BANG, AND OTHER TIMES... WELL.

FOR THE FIRST TIME IN FOUR YEARS, SAMWELL DIDN'T MAKE IT PAST THE FIRST ROUND IN THE ECAC PLAYOFFS.

IT'S KIND OF *HARD* WITHOUT ONE OF THE NHL'S CURRENT TOP SCORERS ON OUR ROSTER, BUT...

OUR CAPTAINS SHOULD HAVE ZERO REGRETS.

OH MAN! *WOW!* REAL FRAT HOUSE!

BITTLE.

MR. ZIMMERMANN.

YOU'RE LUCKY TATER HAS BEEN WANTING TO VISIT THE HAUS FOR MONTHS. WELL, EVER SINCE I TOLD HIM LARDO IS UNBEATABLE AT BEER PONG.

UM, TATER, MAYBE YOU SHOULDN'T BE THROWING THIS ALL UP ON SOCIAL MEDIA...

NO NO! IT'S OKAY! I SHARE PHOTOS TOMORROW, LONG GONE.

17,151 likes   1h ago
a91mashkov Zimmboni College! Go wellies! #samwell #goPVDFalcs

10,333 likes   1h ago
a91mashkov Jam! Thanks aunt judy!! #samwell #goPVDFalcs

12,207 likes   1h ago
a91mashkov PONG GOD!!! #samwell #goPVDFalcs

9,118 likes   1h ago
a91mashkov gross couch! #samwell #goPVDFalcs

WHERE'S RANSOM? #KEAGSTER'S STARTING IN HALF AN HOUR.

15,845 likes   1h ago
a91mashkov Happy Easter!!!

20

C

WELL, Y'ALL!! *THIS IS IT!* WE'RE ALL OFF TO THE END-OF-THE-YEAR BANQUET OUT AT THE SAMWELL GOLF COURSE.

IT'S ONE OF MY FAVORITE EVENTS OF THE SEASON BECAUSE SAMWELL HOCKEY *DOES* CLEAN UP NICE, BUT...

...IT'S SAD.

BECAUSE AFTER THAT, IT'S A *WHIRLWIND*. IT'S THE BANQUET, THEN READING WEEK, THEN FINALS, THEN GRADUATION, AND THEN...

...I WON'T SEE THESE BOYS FOR THE SUMMER.

AND *THEN* I'VE ONLY GOT ONE YEAR LEFT AT SAMWELL UNIVERSITY.

LORD KNOWS I'M NOT ONE TO GET AHEAD OF MYSELF, BUT. *THREE YEARS ALREADY!*

LIFE JUST GOES BY SO *FAST*, Y'KNOW? Y'ALL WERE HERE WHEN I MOVED IN!

I COULDA SWORN I WAS BRINGING A PECAN PIE TO MY FIRST KEGSTER YESTERDAY. AND NOW...

I'LL SAY *THIS*. EVEN WITH ALL OF ITS UPS AND DOWNS, IT'S BEEN A GOOD YEAR.

AND THIS YEAR ESPECIALLY, I'M *SO* PROUD OF WHAT THE TEAM HAS BECOME.

I GUESS IF YOU TOLD ME I WOULD BE— *COULD BE* PART OF A TEAM LIKE THIS AS A FROG, I WOULDN'T HAVE BELIEVED YOU.

MOVING OUT

THE FATE OF OUR RECENT GRADUATES? ADAM AND JUSTIN ARE OFF TO BOSTON TO WORK AS "PROJECT MANAGERS" AT AN APP CONSULTING START-UP.

THEY'LL BE APARTMENT HUNTING NEXT WEEK AND STARTING THE SOULLESS CORPORATE GRIND IN THE FALL.

LARDO WILL **ALSO** BE IN BOSTON—HER HOMETOWN. THE LATEST REPORT IS "HANGING OUT WITH SHITTY I GUESS."

"FIGURING THINGS OUT. MAYBE AN MFA."

...HAUS 2.0, ANYONE?

DUDE! ⇒SNIFF⇐ WE AGREED NO WATERWORKS.

UGH. I'M S-SUCH A BABY.

BUT! GOING TO FALCS' PLAYOFF GAMES WITH THE GANG MAKES IT FEEL LIKE JUNIOR YEAR ISN'T OVER.

AFTER ALL, I'M NOT ON A PLANE BACK TO ATLANTA JUST YET.

I'VE STILL GOT TO TALK TO MY MOTHER ABOUT, UM, SUMMER LODGING WITH MY SIGNIFICANT OTHER.

WE'LL SEE HOW THAT GOES...

CUP I — PLAYOFFS

OR MAYBE *FOCUSED* IS A BETTER WORD. EITHER WAY, I'M PROUD AND IMPRESSED!

AND IT'S GONNA TAKE *EVERYTHING* TO GET TO SIXTEEN WINS.

BUT IT'S JUST LIKE JACK SAID IN HIS POST-GAME INTERVIEW LAST NIGHT— IT'S GONNA BE ONE GAME AT A TIME.

BECAUSE I KNOW THE PRESSURE DOESN'T LET UP UNTIL YOU *HIT* SIXTEEN WINS.

LORD.

ONE GAME.

BITS?

...BITTY?

OH, THERE HE IS! *MONSIEUR GRUMPY,* FRESH FROM NAP TOWN!

AND YOU KNOW I'M IN THE KITCHEN!

SWEETHEART, YOUR PHONE WAS BUZZING FOR A WHOLE MINUTE AND I KNOW IT WASN'T THE GROUP CHAT SINCE—

BITTY.

AND, SLEEPING BEAUTY, YOU WOKE UP JUST IN TIME! I WAS STARTING TO GET LONELY OUT HERE.

WHAT'RE YOU MAKING?

ALMOND BUTTER AND BREAD FOR *THIRTY* PEANUT BUTTER AND JELLY SANDWICHES.

OH! AND I KNOW YOU MUST BE DRAINED SO—

LET ME HELP. IT'D TAKE MY MIND OFF STUFF.

...WELL! THEN COME HELP ME DICE NUTS, YA BIG *LUG*.

HAH... THANKS, BITS.

CUP II —
SUMMER WITH JACK

125

127

24

CUP III — 7 GAMES

Game 1

Game 6

SERIES
3-3 TIE

Game 7

CUP IV —
CENTER ICE

CUP V —
POST

SENIOR YEAR

WAKE-UP CALL

NONSTOP CELLY

PRESSER

JACK, WHAT DOES THE FALCONERS' STATEMENT "PROUD OF ALL INDIVIDUALS WHO MAKE UP OUR TEAM" MEAN?

JACK, HOW ARE PROVIDENCE FALCONERS FANS REACTING TO YOUR ANNOUNCEMENT?

HOW DID YOU FIT INTO THE LOCKER ROOM THIS Y—

WAS THAT KISS YOUR WAY OF COMING OUT AS THE FIRST OPENLY GAY MALE IN A MAJOR LEAGUE SPORT?

HOW DO YOU THINK FANS FROM OPPOSING—

HOW DOES IT FEEL TO WIN A STANLEY CUP AS SUCH A YOUNG TEAM?

NORMAL.

JEEZ, RIGHT OUT THE GATES, EH?

BEFORE WE GET TO ANY OF THAT. I...I THINK I SPEAK FOR EVERYONE IN SAYING WE'RE STILL SO EXCITED COMING OFF THIS HUGE WIN.

LIKE I SAID OUT THERE ON THE ICE, THIS IS REALLY AN INCREDIBLE GROUP OF GUYS.

AND THE SCHOONERS WERE A GREAT TEAM. THEY PUT UP A TOUGH FIGHT TO THE VERY LAST MINUTE.

BUT AT EVERY LEVEL HERE, TOP TO BOTTOM, FROM THE WHOLE ORGANIZATION, WE PUT IN A TEAM EFFORT.

AND WE'RE HAPPY TO HAVE A CUP TO SHOW FOR IT.

<YEAH, IT GOT A LITTLE CRAZY BUT WE WERE MOSTLY AT OUR APARTMENT. HAHA, *YES*, WE'RE VERY RESPONSIBLE.>

<OKAY. WE HAVE PRESS STUFF AFTER THE PARADE BUT WE CAN ALL GET DINNER.>

<BITTY'S STILL HERE. UH...>

<...HE HASN'T TALKED TO THEM YET. NO. YEAH...ME, TOO. OKAY.>

<BYE.>

I PUT A LOT OF STUFF ON PRIVATE YESTERDAY, BUT I TOOK CARE OF SOME OF MY SMALLER ACCOUNTS TODAY.

...SORRY YOU HAVE TO DO THAT.

I DON'T HAVE TO...

BUT I SHOULD CALL HOME.

RIGHT NOW? TONIGHT?

I SHOULD, SHOULDN'T I?

DO YOU KNOW WHAT YOU WANT TO SAY?

...NO.

CALLING HOME

#KUPDAY

HEY, Y'ALL! I WANNA THANK EVERYONE FOR THE OVERWHELMING SUPPORT FOR JACK'S TEAM. FOR SAMWELL HOCKEY.

SO AGAIN, I'LL *BRB* AFTER THINGS SIMMER DOWN A LIL.

...FOR ME.

I'LL BE TAKING A BREAK FROM SOCIAL MEDIA THIS SUMMER... BUT I'LL BE BACK IN THE FALL!

(THOUGH I'LL UPLOAD *JAM FEUD: PART 8 RIGHT* NOW, SINCE I GOT THAT QUEUED UP.)

THANK Y'ALL SO MUCH. I LOVE YOU.

AND IF YOU CAN, MAKE IT OUT TO THE VICTORY PARADE!

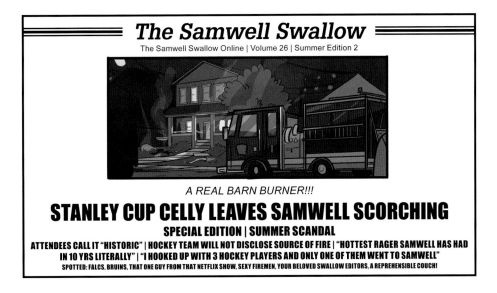

The Samwell Swallow

The Samwell Swallow Online | Volume 26 | Summer Edition 2

A REAL BARN BURNER!!!

STANLEY CUP CELLY LEAVES SAMWELL SCORCHING
SPECIAL EDITION | SUMMER SCANDAL
ATTENDEES CALL IT "HISTORIC" | HOCKEY TEAM WILL NOT DISCLOSE SOURCE OF FIRE | "HOTTEST RAGER SAMWELL HAS HAD IN 10 YRS LITERALLY" | "I HOOKED UP WITH 3 HOCKEY PLAYERS AND ONLY ONE OF THEM WENT TO SAMWELL"
SPOTTED: FALCS, BRUINS, THAT ONE GUY FROM THAT NETFLIX SHOW, SEXY FIREMEN, YOUR BELOVED SWALLOW EDITORS, A REPREHENSIBLE COUCH!

OUR SWEATY NIGHT WITH STANLEY

We here at the *Swallow* remain dedicated to providing you, dear reader, with reports on the juiciest Wellie gossip and coverage on the raunchiest Samwell orgies. Imagine how *beside ourselves* we were, when we learned our favorite (and now gayest!!) alum of our favorite (far from the gayest!!) athletics cult was coming home with the STANLEY CUP.

That's right! **JACK ZIMMERMANN '15**, newly proud and historic gay of the NHL, angst boy, and a **Swallow's 50 Most Gold Star**, returned with some serious hardware. We know most Wellies only watch sports by accident, but even the most reclusive Adderall-riddled biochem major knows that JACK ZIMMERMANN came out on national TV after the Super Bowl. (Basically.)

Our staffers caught several glimpses of the famed Hockey Cup amidst all of the grinding and binge-drinking, and even spotted current hockey captain **ERIC BITTLE '17** with his beau before the two mysteriously disappeared— with the Stanley Cup. Only Lord Stanley knows how his trophy was later *defiled!* Hopefully, not reenacting Jack's first brush with the trophy??? (...Yuck!)

We at the *Swallow* are professional gossipmongers. By the time that one pap showed up, the bacchanalia was over.

Covering college parties? *Well, you're our kind of garbage,* but SMH is our beat, fuck you very much!!

Anonymous Hockey Player Tells All!

"Uh, well, I've been here all summer cuttin' grass and stuff at the golf course?? So it's cool that Jack Zimmermann came by with the Cup and stuff. I got to, like, touch it and stuff??? It's real cool...

"Well, it's cold because it's metal. **I think.** But yeah... then the Kegster kinda just happened. There's my team...the Falcs...I think a lot of these kids go to other schools???

"...Wait, uh, is that a fire on the porch?

"Uh-oh...BITTY-"

VARSITY CAPTAINS

LIFE ISN'T EXACTLY NORMAL, BUT IT'S CALMER. OUR NEW FRESHMEN *(THE WAFFLES)* GOT TO MEET JACK AND IT WAS ONLY A MINOR HOOPLA.

(CAN I JUST SAY—IT'S NICE TO FINALLY BE ABLE TO TALK ABOUT JACK ON A VLOG??? BUT I'LL PROLLY KEEP STICKING TO RECIPES AND TEAM UPDATES!)

(HE *MIGHT* COME ON AS A GUEST IF Y'ALL PROMISE TO *BE CIVIL*.)

PRESEASON IS WELL UNDERWAY AND CLASSES START NEXT WEEK... TRAINING FOR *MY LAST SEASON OF DIVISION ONE HOCKEY*.

LORD, I'M CAPTAIN THIS YEAR. CAPTAIN OF *THE SAMWELL MEN'S HOCKEY TEAM*.

AND BEFORE YOU GO CRAZY IN THE COMMENTS SECTION, I'M NOT PUTTING THAT MUCH PRESSURE ON MYSELF.

(...I THINK.)

IT'S JUST THAT I KNOW I HAVE THE CHANCE TO INSPIRE OTHERS *BY BEING OUT* AND LEADING THIS NCAA DIVISION I TEAM.

...SO HOW DO YOU BE A ROLE MODEL? HOW DO YOU EVEN BE A GOOD CAPTAIN?

179

HAZE BY HAZEWEST: ROOKIE BLANKET

8

HAUS 2.0

WHISKEY

COACH — I

COACH — II

WELL, I'M GLAD I COULD STOP BY BEFORE YOUR WARM-UPS.

IF ANY OF YOUR CREW WANT TO COME WITH TONIGHT—

THERE'S A LITTLE RESTAURANT DOWNTOWN WHERE WE CAN WATCH YOUR FRIEND JACK'S GAME.

SEE YOU, JUNIOR.

BYE, DADDY.

AFTERNOON GAME VS. DARTMOUTH

TANGO, DID YOUR MOM JUST DROP AN F-BOMB ON THE REF?

I LOVE IT.

HAHA, PROBABLY.

TANGO, IF YOUR MOM KEEPS YELLING, IT'LL ACTIVATE MY MOM.

BITTY, WHERE'S YOUR DAD?

THAT'S A SHOT, HOPPER!!

BITTLE, WHISKEY, O'MEARA.

COACH — III

YOU ARE NOT SUPPOSED TO SEE THIS

COACH — IV

14

CHRISTMAS IN MADISON — I

15

CHRISTMAS IN MADISON — II

HE'S REALLY TAKING JACK AROUND TOWN... IT'S NEARLY ONE PM!

THOSE POOR THINGS ARE GONNA MISS OUT ON ALL OUR EGGNOG.

WELL, I KNOW JACK IS ALIVE, HE'S BEEN *TEXTING ME.*

...DICKY.

JUST KIDDING!

JACK CAN SURVIVE A FEW HOURS WITH DADDY UNSUPERVISED...

NO, DICKY...

I'M GLAD YOU BROUGHT JACK HOME.

OH.

OH, WELL, YOU KNOW HOW MUCH HE LOVES MADISON.

NO. NO, I MEAN.

I'M GLAD YOU BROUGHT JACK HOME AS YOUR PARTNER. YOUR BOYRIEND.

YOU KNOW THAT, RIGHT? YOU CAN BRING ANYONE HOME AND YOU WILL STILL HAVE A HOME. NOTHING CAN CHANGE THAT.

WHAT.

HEY. WE'RE BACK FROM THE ST—

WHY'RE Y'ALL ALL *WORKED UP?*

DICKY, YOU KNOW HOW I FEEL ABOUT JUDY'S JAM—YOU WAITED UNTIL CHRISTMAS TO TELL ME—

JUDY AND YOUR COUSINS ARE COMING OVER AND I'M GONNA— I CAN'T BELIEVE SHE WOULD INDOCTRINATE—

BECAUSE I KNEW YOU'D THROW A *FIT!*

OH. IT'S THE JAM.

JUDITH PHELPS, I'D LIKE TO HAVE A WORD ABOUT MY SON AND YOUR PRESERVATION HERESY.

KEEP IT MOVING.

CHRISTMAS
IN MADISON — III

SENIOR THESIS

18

PLAYOFFS

ALMOST EVERY YEAR SINCE JACK ENROLLED IN SAMWELL, SAMWELL MEN'S HOCKEY HAS MADE IT TO THE NCAA PLAYOFFS.

WE'RE SAMWELL. IT'S ALMOST A GIVEN AT THIS POINT.

FIRST OUT CAP

...

IT'S IMPOSSIBLE TO DESCRIBE THAT FEELING OF KNOWING HOW EACH TIME I STEP ONTO THE ICE COULD BE MY LAST.

MY LAST CHANCE TO POUR OUT *EVERYTHING* I CAN FOR MY TEAM—

THESE PEOPLE WHO HAVE GIVEN SO MUCH TO ME.

BUT IT'S NOT JUST ABOUT ME.

IF SAMWELL WINS...IT'S ALMOST LIKE THE CULTURE THAT HAS ALLOWED ME TO BE WHO I AM—WINS.

AND WE CAN SHOW THE COUNTRY THAT. WE CAN SHOW EVERYBODY.

IT'S A LONG ROAD THROUGH THE ECAC TOURNAMENT...TO THE SEMIFINALS.

TO THE FROZEN FOUR...

...TO A CHAMPIONSHIP.

BUT WHILE IT'S ONE GAME AT A TIME...

IT'S ALSO IMPORTANT TO CELEBRATE.

WE'RE HEADING TO REGIONALS, BITCHES!

BIT-TY! BIT-TY! BIT-TY!

YAAAAAH

COME ON, CAPTAIN!!

I'M GETTING TOO OLD FOR THIS.

PARSE

YOU'D TELL HIM SORRY?

YOU CALLED HIM WORTHLESS. AND SAID HE WAS TOO MESSED UP TO CARE ABOUT. AFTER KNOWING HOW HE TOOK TIME OFF BECAUSE— HOW HE ALMOST TOOK HIS OWN—

BECAUSE HE ALMOST BELIEVED HE WASN'T WORTH ANYTHING. *PARSE, YOU SAID THAT TO HIM.*

WHAT?

NO. OR—

I GUESS I OWE JACK AN APOLOGY.

I KNOW THE LAST TIME WE TALKED— HE PROBABLY FORGOT ALL THE SHIT I SAID. NOT LIKE I SAID ANYTHING TERRIBLE.

ACTUALLY, I WAS THERE?

YEAH.

YEAH, I DID SAY THAT. THAT WAS...THERE'S NOT AN EXCUSE FOR THAT.

YEAH.

RIGHT.

SORRY YOU HEARD THAT. OR I MEAN, I'M SORRY *I SAID* THAT.

251

20

SPOTLIGHT ON
ERIC BITTLE

The Samwell men's hockey team is no stranger to the NCAA men's ice hockey playoffs. Since Jack Zimmermann '15 joined the club in 2011, Samwell has enjoyed frequent appearances in the tournament every spring. But with this playoff appearance, another spotlight shines on Samwell hockey, and this light is trained on Eric Bittle '17, the current captain of the men's ice hockey team, who has been in the news for more than just sports. Bittle made headlines last spring when he and Zimmermann shared a history-making kiss at center ice after game 7 of the Stanley Cup playoffs. Now, leading Samwell men's ice hockey to his last NCAA tourney appearance, Bittle is officially the first openly gay Division I men's ice hockey captain in NCAA history.

This is Samwell men's hockey's third time in the NCAA playoffs in four years and second time in the Frozen Four. How does this appearance feel different from past experiences?

Every journey to the playoffs has its own unique challenges, and this season has been no different. But I would definitely say the stakes are higher. I'd be remiss if I didn't attribute those raised stakes to my role as the first openly queer captain of a D-I NCAA men's hockey team, and what a win could mean for queer people everywhere. But other than my personal investment, I'd say we're putting in the same hard work Samwell puts in every year.

In your interview with the *Daily* this October, you talked about being a role model in two ways: as a captain and as a visible queer athlete. Now that Samwell is back on the national stage, your position as a leader has a much larger impact. As your season closes, what do you think you've learned about being a role model?

That it's hard. [*laughs*] As a captain, the number one lesson I've learned is that I'm mostly a teammate/linemate first and that I'm a captain second. It's my job to lead and motivate the team—to be a role model in some respects, but at the end of the day, each of us takes turns pushing each other and supporting each other. It's the same for every game, even a playoff match. And as an openly gay athlete...I think sometimes all you need to be a role model is to exist. To show it can work. Being a role model isn't about being perfect, it's giving an example of one way to live life successfully.

FIRST PERIOD WAS FIRST PERIOD, CHOWDER, COME ON.

JUST CURIOUS AND TOTALLY OFF THE RECORD—

—IT MUST BE HARD TO BE INVESTED IN TWO TEAMS AT THIS POINT?

OH, YOU MEAN KEEPING UP WITH THE FALCS??

OH MY GOODNESS, THEY'VE HAD A ROCKY SEASON. REPEATS ARE SO HARD—BECAUSE WHEN YOU'RE THE CHAMPS TEAMS COME AT YOU THAT MUCH HARDER.

ALSO, YOU HAVE LESS OF AN OFF-SEASON BECAUSE YOU GO ALMOST TWO MONTHS INTO THE PLAYOFFS WHILE MOST OTHER TEAMS ARE RESTING AND ALREADY PREPARING FOR THE NEXT SEASON.

ALSO SNOWY— DUSTIN??? SNOW?? GOT PUT OUT FOR AN INJURY.

SO IN SHORT, YES. I'M WORRIED FOR TWO TEAMS.

I'VE BAKED THEM A TRUCKLOAD OF CHEDDAR AND BLUEBERRY SCONES (FALCS COLORS), AS PER THEIR REQUEST.

WOW. OKAY, ON THE RECORD—

ON THE RECORD!

Samwell men's hockey has been a welcoming space for you, but hockey is not known as the most inclusive sport. Playing against other teams, did you feel a change stepping out onto the ice this season?

In some ways yes, and in some ways no.

More often than not, our opponents didn't seem to care—I was just another Samwell jersey in a play. You'll always get negative comments here and there, and people who target you, but I'm lucky to have teammates who have my back.

What makes Samwell a safe space for queer athletes? And Samwell men's hockey a safe space for you? How can other teams follow suit?

The culture was set way before I got here, and I hope I helped strengthen it. The type of homophobic or misogynistic talk you see in other locker rooms really gets shut down here. Even when I was a freshman some of the seniors would really be firm on that. I think some of the guys took that stance and everyone else followed suit. I think other teams just have to make that the norm. Which might be scary and might get you made fun of—but if everyone has a zero-tolerance stance on those types of comments, no one can complain.

Finally, any advice to queer athletes out there who might be reading this?

LAST DANCE

CHECK

DIBS

TO BE FAIR, I MIGHT HAVE BEEN MILDLY CONCUSSED. BUT STILL.

I WOULD NOT HAVE MISSED IT FOR THE WORLD.

I DON'T REMEMBER A LOT OF THE NEXT 48 HOURS AFTER WINNING.

(NOT BECAUSE I WAS CONCUSSED.)

THERE WERE A LOT OF INTERVIEWS, A LOT OF PARTYING.

A LOT OF CRYING—

—AND A LOT OF JOY.

CLASS DAY

25

FABER

CHECK, PLEASE

THANK YOU.

THANK YOU FOR STICKING WITH ME THROUGH EVERY RECIPE, EVERY REPORT ON MY TEAM.

THROUGH ALL THE HIATUSES AND THROUGH MY CRUSHES AND HEARTACHE. *FOR BEING THERE.*

THANK YOU FOR EVERYTHING YOU'VE GIVEN ME OVER THE LAST FOUR YEARS.

I REALLY LOVE Y'ALL! I DO!

THANK YOU!

AND LAST BUT NOT LEAST, I WANTED TO ANNOUNCE—

THAT I'M WORKING ON A *COOKBOOK!* I JUST GOT THE NEWS ABOUT THE DEAL, AND I'M *SO EXCITED.*

SO IN THESE NEW VLOG UPDATES, Y'ALL'LL GET TO SEE ME WORK ON THIS BOOK IN REAL TIME.

AND WE'RE GONNA JUMP RIGHT INTO IT WITH MY VERY FIRST GUEST!

written & illustrated by

Ngozi Ukazu

with assistance from

**Johel Rivera,
Chelle Finkler,
& Tess Stone**

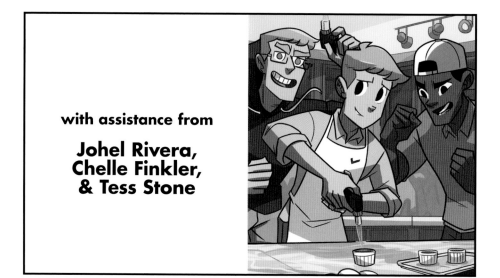

**with special
thanks to**

**Gale Galligan,
Max Ritvo,
Madeline Rupert,
Dave Valeza,
Rachel Young,
and Liam**

This story is dedicated to

my mom & my dad

**And to
every reader**

And to anyone who wants to thrive in a place where the world says they can't.

The End

EXTRA COMICS

LOCKER ROOM

locker room, n.

1. The hallowed ground where the hockey player prepares for battle. What happens amongst the stalls—gross, heinous, or legendary—stays there.

HOCKEY SPEAK

hockey speak, n.

1. The reserved cadence, tone, and
   vocabulary used by hockey players
   during media appearances and
   moments of observed introspection.
   A modern cultural phenomenon.

HOCKEY SPEAK!

- A monotone

- Frequent sighing

- Use of top ten hockey catchphrases

- Interjections of "uh," "you know," "obviously," and "there"

- Immense physical discomfort. Torture.

- Spontaneous Canadian accent

- An empty stare that suggests an inner void

- Focus on team play. Go, team!!

INTERESTINGLY ENOUGH, MOST HOCKEY PLAYERS CAN CODE SWITCH BACK TO REGULAR WHITE-GUY ATHLETIC TALK.

BUT SOME PLAYERS FIND THIS MORE DIFFICULT.

SO, JACK, WHAT FIRST MADE YOU INTERESTED IN BITTY?

⋛SIGH⋚ WELL, OBVIOUSLY HE PLAYS A GREAT GAME. GOOD GUY—SOLID. NOTICED HOW HE PASSED THE PUCK AND BRINGS THE WHOLE TEAM INTO THE PLAY.

UHHH, GREAT QUALITIES FOR A LINEMATE AND PARTNER THERE. SO, YOU KNOW, WE KEPT IT SIMPLE OUT THERE, I THINK, WE TOOK IT ONE SHIFT AT A TIME, AND, YOU KNOW, I TRIED TO BRING MY "A" GAME.

WHAT??

I THOUGHT HE WAS CUTE.

WHEN DID YOU CHANGE INTO YOUR... UNIFORM?

OVERALL, HOCKEY SPEAK IS THE RESULT OF HOCKEY CULTURE. THAT IS, THE LUNCH-PAIL AND TEAM-ORIENTED MENTALITY THAT PROMOTES NOT ONLY WORKING AS A UNIT... BUT INADVERTENTLY SPEAKING AS ONE.

ON THE LINE WE HAVE JOHN JOHNSON, FORMER GOALIE FOR SAMWELL MEN'S HOCKEY. JOHNSON, CAN YOU GIVE US YOUR THOUGHTS ON HOCKEY SPEAK?

PRANKS

TWEETS

SO. It turns out having a Secret NHL Boyfriend changes up how you tweet. First (when no one **knows** you're dating), it makes all your social media communication extremely vague. Second (when all of **America** knows you're dating), it makes you put your entire account on PRIVATE! But you've been keeping up with my vlog for all these years—I want to share my musings from my junior and senior year at Samwell with you! After all, Lardo, Rans, and Holster shouldn't be the only folks reading my tweets. Look out for a new (public!) account from me when my book comes out! 🏒✓♥

Eric Bittle @omgcheckplease · Thursday, August 27, 2015 | 3:12 PM

Well. It's about time I tackled my language requirement at Samwell. (Bonjour?)

Eric Bittle @omgcheckplease · Friday, September 4, 2015 | 2:33 PM

Shitty just group texted us a picture of his study carrel in the library w/ the caption "JUST MOVED IN!!!!" ;~; Let this law student survive.

Eric Bittle @omgcheckplease · Friday, September 4, 2015 | 6:23 PM

Rans: how come jack hasn't introduced us to mashkov yet? he owes us! right??
Holster: he totally owes us. hashtag Mashkov kegster 2015

Eric Bittle @omgcheckplease · Friday, September 4, 2015 | 8:04 PM

Rans: I bet he's SO good at pong
Holster: and probably like a tank
(R&H still talking about Alexei Mashkov)

Eric Bittle @omgcheckplease · Monday, September 7, 2015 | 2:33 PM

We're getting a visitor later today!!!!! so I HAVE to finish these PIES.

Eric Bittle @omgcheckplease · Monday, September 7, 2015 | 2:57 PM

Ransom: oh BRO BRO maybe he'll bring Mashkov
Holster: [LOUD GASP] TEXT HIM

Eric Bittle @omgcheckplease · Monday, September 7, 2015 | 4:46 PM

Jack: Yeah, Tater wanted to come. Ah, mashkov. That's what we call him.
Ransom and Holster just said "Tater" in unison, completely in awe.

Eric Bittle @omgcheckplease · Monday, September 7, 2015 | 5:12 PM

Jack: The biggest change is probably my diet. Less pie.
This boy still thinks he's hilarious.

Eric Bittle @omgcheckplease · Thursday, September 10, 2015 | 4:20 AM

merci...more like lord have mercy i just want to go to sleep and stop learning nouns

Eric Bittle @omgcheckplease · Thursday, September 17, 2015 | 6:20 PM

SMH group text
Ransom: yo why haven't we met Mashkov yet?
Jack: maybe after the game
Ransom: oh fuck
Jack: no promises
Ransom: ???????????

Eric Bittle @omgcheckplease · Thursday, September 17, 2015 | 6:23 PM

Ransom: what if he's lame
Ransom: haha impossible

Eric Bittle @omgcheckplease · Wednesday, September 23, 2015 | 9:51 PM

My mother LOVES Shitty's new haircut by the way. Every time I
mention it to her she sighs and goes "you know, thank goodness."

Eric Bittle @omgcheckplease · Friday, October 2, 2015 | 1:11 AM

Me and Lardo just Skyped Shitty! Who actually just Skyped jack.
Who Chowder apparently texted before running into me in the hall.
#connected

Eric Bittle @omgcheckplease · Friday, October 2, 2015 | 1:14 AM

Shitty: Also, Jack Zimmermann has a fucking girlfriend and he's
being cagey about it and it's driving me NUTS

Eric Bittle @omgcheckplease · Saturday, October 3, 2015 | 2:58 PM

Tango: ...that pie was...like, really good. Do you like cook a lot or
something?
Oh my God. Well. Bless his heart.

Eric Bittle @omgcheckplease · Sunday, October 4, 2015 | 2:02 PM

ahem A Tango Follow up
Tango: Bitty should be on TV!
Chowder: Yeah!!!!
Tango: I mean on a TV show.
Chowder: ...Okay!
????

Eric Bittle @omgcheckplease · Friday, October 16, 2015 | 8:26 PM

Re: The Great British Bakeoff!!

Holster: Sweet. I thought I was running out of TV.

Me: Sit down, Tango. You need to be educated.

Tango: huh?

Eric Bittle @omgcheckplease · Friday, October 16, 2015 | 8:27 PM

....And Whiskey, of course, has something else he needs to do. I get it. He doesn't like baking.

Eric Bittle @omgcheckplease · Monday, November 2, 2015 | 1:14 AM

What do I have to do to get Whiskey to spend some time with us? Seriously.

Eric Bittle @omgcheckplease · Tuesday, November 3, 2015 | 9:43 AM

Also, Whiskey said I had a "pretty great shot" after practice. First thing that tadpole's said to me in days! I should be so relieved. These tadpoles are so different from my frogs.

Eric Bittle @omgcheckplease · Wednesday, November 4, 2015 | 7:10 AM

Team Bfast: Post-Grad Employment

Ransom: what if I did consulting

Nursey: you'd be totally soulless and working for the man

Ransom: ...what if I did consulting

Eric Bittle @omgcheckplease · Wednesday, November 4, 2015 | 8:15 PM

I love that Shitty has a naturally curious mind but I really wish he'd, uh, quit trying to figure out who Jack is dating. They're best friends but—privacy? Boundaries?

Eric Bittle @omgcheckplease · Thursday, November 5, 2015 | 3:35 AM

I hate being away from the people I need most. I'm not that strong. Or I know I can and should be stronger. But.

Eric Bittle @omgcheckplease · Thursday, November 5, 2015 | 3:41 AM

There's so many things I can't do and can't say. So many secrets and it's so unfair. I'm just going to finish this pile of flashcards and go to bed.

Eric Bittle @omgcheckplease · Thursday, November 5, 2015 | 1:46 PM

Good job last night, Falconers.

Eric Bittle @omgcheckplease · Thursday, November 5, 2015 | 4:51 PM

Hanging out in the kitchen
Lardo: well.
Lardo: gotta start looking for a new team manager
Dex: W-WAIT YOU HAVEN'T STARTED TRAINING SOMEONE

Eric Bittle @omgcheckplease · Thursday, November 5, 2015 | 4:51 PM

Dex: they have to know our schedules—practice times, game times—GAME DAY PROCEDURE—locker room rules, equipment organization, THE BYLAWS
This is amazing. He's really freaking out.

Eric Bittle @omgcheckplease · Thursday, November 5, 2015 | 4:56 PM

I think lardo could assuage his fears,
But she's enjoying this

Eric Bittle @omgcheckplease · Thursday, November 5, 2015 | 4:59 PM

Chowder: helloooo! Mmm!!! are those brownies??
Dex: lardo's looking for her replacement
Chowder: i don't want a brownie anymore :((((

Eric Bittle @omgcheckplease · Thursday, November 5, 2015 | 5:02 PM

Nursey: oh shit brownies
Chowder: Lardo's finding another manager for us!
Nursey: augff! Aawwwff larffo!

Eric Bittle @omgcheckplease · Friday, November 13, 2015 | 8:50 PM

Chowder's interior design approach is "What would happen if the San Jose Sharks gift shop exploded?"

Eric Bittle @omgcheckplease · Sunday, November 22, 2015 | 1:22 PM

Waiting for the boys at Jerry's with Jack. (Yes, it's true, they serve brunch.)

Eric Bittle @omgcheckplease · Sunday, November 22, 2015 | 1:31 PM

When you tell your teammates about your SO because you trust and love them.
And they respond with an endless torrent of chirps. #SMH

Eric Bittle @omgcheckplease · Tuesday, November 24, 2015 | 9:02 PM

- SMH Group Text -
Shitty: Sooooooo
Shitty: heard Bitty's new piece is slammin'
Ransom: lol oh ya bro
Ransom: Bitty's got mad wheels

Eric Bittle @omgcheckplease · Tuesday, November 24, 2015 | 9:07 PM

Jack: This is a Samwell hockey record
Jack: Chirps lasting longer than the ones re: Holster & Esther S.
Shitty: HooAOHAHFUCK
Holster: ... Jack

Eric Bittle @omgcheckplease · Tuesday, November 24, 2015 | 9:08 PM

Jack: :)
Holster: Don't fucking smiley face at me when you threw me under the bus
Holster: why you come for me like that, man?

Eric Bittle @omgcheckplease · Tuesday, November 24, 2015 | 9:13 PM

Nursey: whos ES
Jack: i'll write you an email
Holster: AN EMAIL?? REALLY??
Holster: I DIDN'T EVEN START THIS

Eric Bittle @omgcheckplease · Friday, December 4, 2015 | 12:54 AM

Dear Bittle's followers,
Bittle has exams and needed help studying for them. He revoked his Twitter privileges until he passes French.

Eric Bittle @omgcheckplease · Friday, December 4, 2015 | 12:55 AM

And reviews for his HIST exam. And finishes his essay for prof. Atley's Indep. study.

Eric Bittle @omgcheckplease · Friday, December 4, 2015 | 12:56 AM

He says "Sorry, y'all! Gotta buckle down!...I'm gonna regret this."

Eric Bittle @omgcheckplease · Friday, December 4, 2015 | 12:56 AM

He will be fine. He promises to study hard. Thanks.

Eric Bittle @omgcheckplease · Monday, December 7, 2015 | 1:02 PM
Have been told to tweet "#GoPVDFalconers".

Eric Bittle @omgcheckplease · Thursday, December 10, 2015 | 10:51 PM
Update: studying well, excited for jam in GA...Aunt Judy's jam.

Eric Bittle @omgcheckplease · Saturday, December 12, 2015 | 7:26 AM
Epikegster planning. #Epikegster

Eric Bittle @omgcheckplease · Wednesday, December 16, 2015 | 4:02 AM
Samwell has one more game left in 2015. #samwellhockey

Eric Bittle @omgcheckplease · Wednesday, December 16, 2015 | 4:04 AM
Overall doing good .PCT
all games: .583
conference: .500
The boys can build up momentum. #samwellhockey

Eric Bittle @omgcheckplease · Wednesday, December 16, 2015 | 4:05 AM
We always have a good showing in the spring. #samwellhockey
#samwell

Eric Bittle @omgcheckplease · Wednesday, December 16, 2015 | 4:06 AM
Bittle's up late for a paper due tomorrow at noon.

Eric Bittle @omgcheckplease · Wednesday, December 16, 2015 | 4:11 AM
Will pass on encouragement, thanks!

Eric Bittle @omgcheckplease · Wednesday, December 16, 2015 | 3:26 PM
Good play but tough losses.

Eric Bittle @omgcheckplease · Wednesday, December 16, 2015 | 4:22 PM
Finish that paper, Bittle! Let's go! Home stretch. French next.

Eric Bittle @omgcheckplease · Thursday, December 17, 2015 | 8:23 AM
Presentation finale.

Eric Bittle @omgcheckplease · Thursday, December 17, 2015 | 9:07 AM

DONE!!

Eric Bittle @omgcheckplease · Thursday, December 17, 2015 | 9:13 AM

I would like to thank my very incredible ghost-tweeter for keeping everyone updated!

Eric Bittle @omgcheckplease · Friday, December 25, 2015 | 5:45 AM

Merry Christmas, y'all!

Eric Bittle @omgcheckplease · Saturday, December 26, 2015 | 12:33 AM

- SMH Group Text -
Jack: Excited for boxing day.
Holster: Jack you do this joke every year.

Eric Bittle @omgcheckplease · Monday, December 28, 2015 | 9:35 PM

Dex: hey, Tango, what're you thinking about majoring in?
Tango: hm.
Tango: CS seems pretty easy so far
Dex: [spits out pie]

Eric Bittle @omgcheckplease · Monday, December 28, 2015 | 9:37 PM

Chowder: What about you, Whisk—
Whiskey: Economics.
Whiskey: I figure I'm playing hockey or doing finance so.

Eric Bittle @omgcheckplease · Monday, December 28, 2015 | 9:40 PM

Chowder: wow, so you think that'll be fun? Or cool?
Whiskey: [shrug]

Eric Bittle @omgcheckplease · Monday, December 28, 2015 | 9:41 PM

I've never seen someone communicate "my decisions are practical, efficient, and probably hereditary" in a shrug

Eric Bittle @omgcheckplease · Sunday, January 3, 2016 | 11:24 PM

- SMH Group Text -
Lardo: officially posted the app for new team manager
Holster: well
Rans: wooow
Nursey: yo
Chowder: :(
Jack: good luck

Eric Bittle @omgcheckplease · Sunday, January 3, 2016 | 11:25 PM

Dex: How many rounds of interviews are you doing?
Dex: I think four is a reasonable number.

Eric Bittle @omgcheckplease · Monday, January 4, 2016 | 1:18 AM

- SMH Group Text -
Nursey: Yo, Bitty do you remember any French?
Jack: no.

Eric Bittle @omgcheckplease · Monday, January 4, 2016 | 1:28 AM

Me: I can speak for myself, Mr. Zimmermann.
Jack: Well.
Jack: Not in French.
Shitty: HAH.

Eric Bittle @omgcheckplease · Tuesday, January 5, 2016 | 1:07 PM

Walking Out of Faber
Nursey: Dex, man, even if our next manager isn't great we can look out for ourselves.
Nursey: [topples down stairs]

Eric Bittle @omgcheckplease · Wednesday, January 13, 2016 | 9:18 PM

- SMH Group Text -
Jack: Anyone watch the #SOTU?
Ransom: I'm studying and Canadian.

Eric Bittle @omgcheckplease · Thursday, January 14, 2016 | 3:05 PM

Whenever I need to use an accented "é" I honestly just Google Beyoncé and copy/paste. #ThoughtsDuringLecture

Eric Bittle @omgcheckplease · Sunday, January 17, 2016 | 3:28 AM

Overheard at a Samwell kegster:
Girl 1: This is like, nice for a frat Haus
Girl 2: You should see the ones in TX
Girl 1: I mean but curtains

Eric Bittle @omgcheckplease · Wednesday, January 20, 2016 | 1:55 PM

I haven't had the chance to talk to this girl yet, but Lardo is training a new manager!

Eric Bittle @omgcheckplease · Thursday, February 4, 2016 | 9:21 AM

Overheard From Across The Hall
Lardo: Chowder. There's white people hair in our shower drain.
Chowder: HOW??????

Eric Bittle @omgcheckplease · Thursday, February 4, 2016 | 10:22 AM

- Busing our breakfast Later-
Chowder: You know? Maybe it's because we're both dating white people?
Lardo: ....mmmmoh yeah.

Eric Bittle @omgcheckplease · Thursday, February 4, 2016 | 4:12 PM

Ford: And what's Kent Parson like?
Me:
Me: He's a hockey player.

Eric Bittle @omgcheckplease · Sunday, February 14, 2016 | 7:50 PM

And happy birthday Derek Nurse! You being born today kind of explains everything

Eric Bittle @omgcheckplease · Monday, February 15, 2016 | 8:10 PM

Nursey: Guess how many cards I got today, Poindexter?
Dex: [a long sigh]
Dex: Like 20.
Nursey: Eight. One was from my mom.

Eric Bittle @omgcheckplease · Monday, February 15, 2016 | 8:11 PM

Ah, Dex tried to hide that laugh but there's pie everywhere.

Eric Bittle @omgcheckplease · Tuesday, March 1, 2016 | 6:53 PM

Lardo's coaching Ford! Personally? I'd teach the finer workings of Samwell hockey anywhere but on that upholstered cesspool we call a couch, but I trust Lardo.

Eric Bittle @omgcheckplease · Tuesday, March 1, 2016 | 6:55 PM

Lardo: And if someone's late you just write it down. If someone doesn't show let RH know.
Ford: RH. RansomHolster. Got it.
Lardo: 'swawes.

Eric Bittle @omgcheckplease · Tuesday, March 1, 2016 | 6:57 PM

Ford: Right. I get that it's positive? But why do you guys say 'swawesome?
Me: You'll find something weirder to worry about soon enough.

Eric Bittle @omgcheckplease · Wednesday, March 2, 2016 | 2:22 PM

Nursey: Hey, Las Vegas is playing Providence tonight.
Dex: Uh oh. Jack versus Parse.
Dex: I'm obvs rooting for Jack but that should be good.

Eric Bittle @omgcheckplease · Thursday, March 3, 2016 | 9:30 PM

NHL players like pie—but also mason jars filled w/ jam prepared according to an old family & aunt-perfected recipe. (A lil bird told me.)

Eric Bittle @omgcheckplease · Thursday, March 3, 2016 | 9:31 PM

But when your #friend asks you to make a batch, does he mean enough for his team? Does that include the coaching staff?

Eric Bittle @omgcheckplease · Wednesday, March 16, 2016 | 6:15 PM

Dear Lord the SMH group chat
Lardo: I need to beat Alexei Mashkov at beer pong.

Eric Bittle @omgcheckplease · Wednesday, March 16, 2016 | 6:17 PM

Jack: haha he's serious about that.
Lardo: then why has it taken so long
Lardo: time and place
Shitty: yessss that's my girl

Eric Bittle @omgcheckplease · Wednesday, March 16, 2016 | 6:18 PM

Tater is literally twice the mass of Larissa Duan.

Eric Bittle @omgcheckplease · Wednesday, March 23, 2016 | 3:42 PM

JAM IS IN DEMAND. The situation: A friend of a friend got hold of my aunt's jam, & now a good portion of a pro. hockey team is on a jam (or pie) waitlist. Odd.

Eric Bittle @omgcheckplease · Friday, March 25, 2016 | 1:12 AM

Coach: How's school?
Me: My GPA's at [OMITTED], meeting w/ my American Studies adviser on my thesis
Coach: History?
Me:
Me: Pie history.

Eric Bittle @omgcheckplease · Friday, March 25, 2016 | 2:29 PM

Holster: what ever happened to the better bitty's butt thing or whatever?
Ransom: oh the bureau? i'm not saying we achieved goals but.

Eric Bittle @omgcheckplease · Friday, March 25, 2016 | 2:33 PM

Ahem Though not much has changed I feel more confident in my assets. It was about bettering the bitty and not the booty all along.

Eric Bittle @omgcheckplease · Friday, March 25, 2016 | 6:19 PM

Ford is a natural. She just sent an email out to the team. Good CHOICE, Lardy-lards!

Eric Bittle @omgcheckplease · Wednesday, March 30, 2016 | 12:28 AM

Half a dozen teams are already guaranteed a spot in the NHL playoffs. The Falconers just joined them #GoPVDFalconers #PVDFalconers #GoFalcs!!!!

Eric Bittle @omgcheckplease · Wednesday, March 30, 2016 | 12:31 AM

- SMH Group Text -
Lardo: you did it you did it you did it you did it you did it you did it you did it you did it you did it you did it you

---

Eric Bittle @omgcheckplease · Tuesday, May 3, 2016 | 3:12 PM

Alice: We'll hit the ground running next year with that thesis!
Me: Yup! I'm going to bake so many pies!!
Alice: child

Eric Bittle @omgcheckplease · Thursday, May 5, 2016 | 9:39 AM
We had an awful lot of "scheming" going on last year for my birthday. I love a surprise every now & then, but I'm glad things seem normal?

Eric Bittle @omgcheckplease · Thursday, May 5, 2016 | 9:52 AM
So. Sometimes when Holster hugs you he'll lift you clean off the ground.

Eric Bittle @omgcheckplease · Thursday, May 5, 2016 | 12:33 PM
Oh my goodness, everyone is so excited today!!! Dex just gave me the biggest hug!!!!! Right off the ground!! He's usually more reserved?...Aw, I'm tearing up.

Eric Bittle @omgcheckplease · Thursday, May 5, 2016 | 12:36 PM
I mean—We were in the middle of the crosswalk at the bridge? He couldn't even wait! A car honked at us, but they don't understand my team.

Eric Bittle @omgcheckplease · Thursday, May 5, 2016 | 1:46 PM
OKAY WHAT

Eric Bittle @omgcheckplease · Thursday, May 5, 2016 | 1:47 PM
I just saw Nursey on River Quad w/ his classmates??
Nursey: ya just a sec
Nursey: Happy Birthday Bitty
NURSEY: [PICKS ME @OMGCHECKPLEASE UP]

Eric Bittle @omgcheckplease · Thursday, May 5, 2016 | 1:50 PM
Wellie: oh my god MOVE i have to turn in this ESSAY
Nursey: haha you need a hug too?
Me: >:(((((

Eric Bittle @omgcheckplease · Thursday, May 5, 2016 | 1:52 PM
...I haven't even seen half my team today

Eric Bittle @omgcheckplease · Thursday, May 5, 2016 | 3:35 PM
Whiskey: Hey, Bitty
Whiskey: [picks me up]
Whiskey: See ya

Eric Bittle @omgcheckplease · Thursday, May 5, 2016 | 3:50 PM

THE GROUP TEXT!!!!!

Holster: Bitty, want to meet for coffee? A lil pick-me-up?

Nursey: I duno bits seems so uplifted today

Eric Bittle @omgcheckplease · Thursday, May 5, 2016 | 3:51 PM

Which one.....

Which one of those boys....................................idea was this......

Eric Bittle @omgcheckplease · Thursday, May 5, 2016 | 3:52 PM

I have to swing by the rink to meet up with Coach Murray—if Lardo is there, she'll illuminate me.

Eric Bittle @omgcheckplease · Thursday, May 5, 2016 | 4:05 PM

Well I just.

Apparently Chowder was working with the goalie coach today.

Chowder: BITTY!!!!!!!!!!!!!!!!!!

Me: [runs]

Eric Bittle @omgcheckplease · Thursday, May 5, 2016 | 4:06 PM

Chowder: [after putting me down] there ya go!

Chowder: I was worried you'd lock yourself in your room!

Chowder: Have a nice birthday!!!!!!!

Eric Bittle @omgcheckplease · Thursday, May 5, 2016 | 5:16 PM

Me: Lardo! I—

Lardo: Hold on.

Me: No.

Lardo: Yes.

Me: You can't.

Lardo: Lol brah.

Lardo: You're not the first

Lardo: not the last

Eric Bittle @omgcheckplease · Thursday, May 5, 2016 | 5:35 PM

Tango: hey

Tango: [picks me up]

Tango: i'm just following orders

Eric Bittle @omgcheckplease · Thursday, May 5, 2016 | 7:01 PM

I hope they're not planning anything crazy downstairs. I specifically requested NO KEGSTERS for my 21st.

Eric Bittle @omgcheckplease · Thursday, May 5, 2016 | 8:31 PM

Y'all, they baked for me.

Eric Bittle @omgcheckplease · Friday, May 13, 2016 | 3:37 PM

Tango: well, I gotta go, but I wanted to say bye, Bitty.
Tango: Bye, Bitty. I had a great year!
I'm gonna cry.

Eric Bittle @omgcheckplease · Wednesday, May 18, 2016 | 6:10 PM

We're on our way to Providence! (And they're already setting chairs up on River Quad.)

Eric Bittle @omgcheckplease · Sunday, May 22, 2016 | 12:28 PM

I'm so proud of my teammates and can't wait to celebrate their accomplishments this weekend. <3 Congrats Samwell 2016!

Eric Bittle @omgcheckplease · Tuesday, June 7, 2016 | 12:28 AM

#GoPVDFalconers!!

Eric Bittle @omgcheckplease · Monday, June 13, 2016 | 8:56 AM

OKAY LOCKED

Eric Bittle @omgcheckplease · Monday, June 13, 2016 | 8:56 AM

ME AND JACK KISSED ON TV

Eric Bittle @omgcheckplease · Saturday, June 18, 2016 | 10:31 AM

The last 5 days have been joyous, insane, chaotic and if i'm being totally honest—mildly terrifying. Thread forthcoming. Lord in heaven.

Eric Bittle @omgcheckplease · Saturday, June 18, 2016 | 10:31 AM

First, I put my Twitter on private a few days ago. Because? ….Y'all, I was getting overwhelmed. If you're still following this account, it means I still *WANT* you following it…

Eric Bittle @omgcheckplease · Saturday, June 18, 2016 | 10:32 AM

(I did a LOT of unfollowing. If you're wondering who all can see this, it's anyone who has lived/is living in the Haus and a handful of baking mutuals. LOCKED DOWN.)

Eric Bittle @omgcheckplease · Saturday, June 18, 2016 | 10:32 AM

Second, I...don't know when I'll unlock this account. If ever. But for now I just want to tweet about me and Jack and SMH and the cup and baking and avoiding my parents

Eric Bittle @omgcheckplease · Saturday, June 18, 2016 | 10:33 AM

Third, I came out to my parents. Kind of. Anyway pie.

Eric Bittle @omgcheckplease · Sunday, June 19, 2016 | 4:19 PM

AND FINALLY I CAN TWEET ABOUT THE FALCS. ONE of WHOM is my BOYFRIEND. JACK ZIMMERMANN. Another of whom is living in my boyfriends condo? ALEXEI MASHKOV.

Eric Bittle @omgcheckplease · Sunday, June 19, 2016 | 4:20 PM

I'm an active member of 5 distinct group chats however. And since many of you are members of those group chats, forgive me for tweeting less.

Eric Bittle @omgcheckplease · Saturday, July 2, 2016 | 11:01 AM

I cannot believe that the Stanley Cup will be in this derelict frat den in a matter of minutes. I am so proud. Haus Sweet Haus!

Eric Bittle @omgcheckplease · Saturday, July 2, 2016 | 12:08 PM

Shitty: Jack
Shitty: Will you please sit in the cup.
Jack: Ah. That's okay

Eric Bittle @omgcheckplease · Saturday, July 2, 2016 | 12:19 PM

Lardo: Tub Juice in the Cup?
Ransom: Tub Juice in the Cup?
Holster: Tub Juice in the CUP?!?
Shitty: TUB JUICE IN THE GODDAMN CUP!!!

Eric Bittle @omgcheckplease · Saturday, July 2, 2016 | 9:19 PM

Well, the Haus is on fire!!!

Eric Bittle @omgcheckplease · Sunday, July 10, 2016 | 10:17 AM

I'm in Providence!

Eric Bittle @omgcheckplease · Sunday, July 10, 2016 | 10:23 AM

I love my boyfriend. How did I spend an entire year VAGUE TWEETING about him. Why didn't y'all stop me. Lord, how tacky.

Eric Bittle @omgcheckplease · Monday, July 11, 2016 | 3:25 PM

Hockey Champion Jack Laurent Zimmermann: I think I'm gonna make an instagram
Me: !!!
HCJLZ: And learn Photoshop
Me: I'm calling the police

Eric Bittle @omgcheckplease · Sunday, August 7, 2016 | 6:00 PM

Lord in heaven, school starts in a week and I owe 18 hockey players—only 40% of whom are falcs—SEVERAL jars of jam.

Eric Bittle @omgcheckplease · Monday, August 8, 2016 | 11:11 AM

The Real Secret For This Secret Twitter: I'm using my aunt's jam recipe. I'm using my Aunt Judy's Recipe and my mother must NEVER know.

Eric Bittle @omgcheckplease · Monday, August 8, 2016 | 11:14 AM

@lemonitswed. Good Question. Back when they were teens, my aunt revamped my grand-moo-maw's recipe and entered the county fair. TO COMPETE WITH MY MAMA.

Eric Bittle @omgcheckplease · Monday, August 8, 2016 | 11:14 AM

My mama had won last year, but aunt judy claims it was 'cause a judge had a crush on my mom? But this year they TIED.
By a HAIR. AND!!!!

Eric Bittle @omgcheckplease · Monday, August 8, 2016 | 11:15 AM

My mama borrowed the only copy of my grand-moo-maw's handwritten jam recipe? And claims that Aunt Judy stole/destroyed it. Aunt Judy denies this...I don't know who to believe.

Eric Bittle @omgcheckplease · Monday, August 8, 2016 | 11:19 AM

the jam feud is the culmination of a decade-long teenage sibling rivalry and southern women weaponizing food preparation.

Eric Bittle @omgcheckplease · Saturday, August 13, 2016 | 7:23 AM
Have you met me and my boyfriend's unexpected injured NHL roommate Alexei Mashkov.
Tater: I move back to my house after summer! No worries! Zimmboni and Pie. Good recovery!

Eric Bittle @omgcheckplease · Tuesday, August 16, 2016 | 1:53 PM
I would never have guessed that Ford, Tango, and Connor would be such good friends, but these frosh groups are unpredictable now, aren't they?

Eric Bittle @omgcheckplease · Tuesday, August 16, 2016 | 1:56 PM
I've broken it down this way: Ford navigates, Whiskey keeps things calm, and Tango keeps things moving. It's really rather sweet. :)

Eric Bittle @omgcheckplease · Thursday, August 18, 2016 | 5:38 PM
Imagine being a freshman on the Samwell men's hockey team and entering into the chaotic media aftermath of your captain kissing Jack Zimmermann on national TV.

Eric Bittle @omgcheckplease · Saturday, August 20, 2016 | 6:10 PM
Imagine being the caPTAIN OF THE SAMWELL MEN'S HOCKEY TEAM AND ENTERING INTO THE CHAOTIC—

Eric Bittle @omgcheckplease · Wednesday, August 24, 2016 | 11:34 AM
@lemonitswed @justincoco91 Why did y'all avoid the captains meetings? I need an answer other than because SMH is an insular cult. I already know this!!

Eric Bittle @omgcheckplease · Wednesday, August 24, 2016 | 11:35 AM
@lemonitswed @justincoco91 Listen, I'm actually going to go to the varsity captains meeting. I need gay friends.

Eric Bittle @omgcheckplease · Wednesday, August 24, 2016 | 1:03 PM
Gays attained.

Eric Bittle @omgcheckplease · Wednesday, August 24, 2016 | 7:31 PM
@ducksducksducksducks @shrutitootie Twitter give me a lesbian flag emoji now, you cowards.

Eric Bittle @omgcheckplease · Monday, October 3, 2016 | 8:45 PM
SORRY SORRY SORRY! For the lack of tweets!! After the start of
OUR season and JACK'S season things got hectic. Nursey broke
his ARM. Ugh!!

Eric Bittle @omgcheckplease · Monday, October 3, 2016 | 11:16 PM
And now I'm mostly tweeting to avoid becoming enraged because I
have to get these freshman OUT of this party.

Eric Bittle @omgcheckplease · Tuesday, October 4, 2016 | 3:06 AM
I think I'm having the worst night I ever had at Samwell.

Eric Bittle @omgcheckplease · Wednesday, October 12, 2016 | 6:52 AM
I cannot stress how important it was for me to be able to choose
when I came out and to who. I don't take that lightly.

Eric Bittle @omgcheckplease · Wednesday, October 12, 2016 | 6:53 AM
And, for me, I needed to feel comfortable. It's scary. There's never
a rush, but finding people who you trust and accept you is
important.

Eric Bittle @omgcheckplease · Wednesday, October 12, 2016 | 9:15 AM
And I just found out my mom can't make it to family weekend so
it's just going to be my dad.

Eric Bittle @omgcheckplease · Saturday, October 15, 2016 | 12:02 AM
Late night walk to Murder Stop N Shop because I have no self-
preservation and I need to stress bake 3 pies

Eric Bittle @omgcheckplease · Monday, October 17, 2016 | 3:26 PM
Visit with Coach: 3/5. We yelled at each other and I cried, but we
had a hug that lasted more than 3 seconds and Jack is coming to
Madison???

Eric Bittle @omgcheckplease · Monday, October 17, 2016 | 4:27 PM
MY BOYFRIEND IS MEETING MY PARENTS ALDFJA;JF;

Eric Bittle @omgcheckplease · Thursday, October 27, 2016 | 8:08 AM
Tuning right on in to Twitter for the inside scoop on the
PROVIDENCE FALCONERS HALLOWEEN PARTY.

Eric Bittle @omgcheckplease · Thursday, November 17, 2016 | 1:04 PM

Listen, I'm not tweeting about politics. I can't. I'm just focusing on hockey and baking and my team.

Eric Bittle @omgcheckplease · Monday, November 21, 2016 | 9:14 AM

Anyway glad I'm staying in Samwell for Thanksgiving. :^)))) I'm pretty sure I'm suffering from mild depression.

Eric Bittle @omgcheckplease · Thursday, December 22, 2016 | 12:35 PM

Jack, getting into my car at Hartsfield-Jackson. "It's two days from Christmas and it's 78 degrees outside." Welcome to Georgia you sweet Canadian nomad.

Eric Bittle @omgcheckplease · Saturday, December 24, 2016 | 10:32 AM

I TOLD MY MOTHER ABOUT THE JAM AND NOW THERE ARE CHRISTMAS TREE COOKIES ON THE CEILING.

Eric Bittle @omgcheckplease · Saturday, December 24, 2016 | 10:35 AM

@lemonitswed - WE WERE SHARING, BIRKHOLTZ @ducksducksducksducks I'll make sure Jack gets some hi-res photos. It's still up on the ceiling. Definitely art.

Eric Bittle @omgcheckplease · Sunday, December 25, 2016 | 9:35 AM

Merry Christmas!! Jack worked up the courage to hug me in front of my dad and no one died, so HAPPY HOLIDAYS

Eric Bittle @omgcheckplease · Sunday, December 25, 2016 | 4:35 PM

You know, kudos to Jack and my dad for having an hour long conversation about soccer. They only talk about sports, history, and rock/country music.

Eric Bittle @omgcheckplease · Sunday, January 1, 2017 | 12:15 AM

Happy New Years!!!

Eric Bittle @omgcheckplease · Friday, January 13, 2017 | 7:00 AM

Hi, I'm back to vent and muse please join me I feel like there's an entire genre of Jock that is probably-bi guys who have no idea what to do with their sexuality

Eric Bittle @omgcheckplease · Friday, January 13, 2017 | 7:03 AM

I realize that everyone has 110% the right to live their lives however they want? But I don't think that one's frustrations with their OWN sexuality—

Eric Bittle @omgcheckplease · Friday, January 13, 2017 | 7:04 AM

Should manifest as disdain for those who feel comfortable in themselves. And that's my tweet. Samwell jocks figure yourselves out. I'm sick of it.

Eric Bittle @omgcheckplease · Tuesday, February 14, 2017 | 8:55 AM

Nursey: Singing Valentine's. Pft. A cappella culture is lowkey lame
Bully: I like a capella
Nursey: i mean it's lame but in a cool way, obviously. So cool.

Eric Bittle @omgcheckplease · Wednesday, February 15, 2017 | 7:43 AM

For a Belated Valentine's Day Gift, Jack drove down to have dinner with the team and the Haus

Eric Bittle @omgcheckplease · Wednesday, February 15, 2017 | 7:47 AM

Because the greatest gift this man can give me is inflicting small, surreptitous but potent amounts of PDA on this hockey team.

Eric Bittle @omgcheckplease · Sunday, February 26, 2017 | 8:12 PM

My friends and family are beginning to become "concerned" about my "lack of progress" on my "senior thesis" and while I appreciate their concern it is most unwanted thank you.

Eric Bittle @omgcheckplease · Monday, February 27, 2017 | 7:30 PM

Hi, it's Jack. Bitty needs to revise his senior thesis. Actually he needs to turn in a draft and then revise that. He's unbelievably behind.

Eric Bittle @omgcheckplease · Tuesday, February 28, 2017 | 7:31 PM

Bitty thought it would be a good idea to change his password until he's done. I'll send updates over the next few weeks.

Eric Bittle @omgcheckplease · Wednesday, March 15, 2017 | 7:54 AM

Samwell's doing well in the playoffs. Some nail biters, but they're pulling through. Bitty had a goal and an assist yesterday against Quinnipiac.

Eric Bittle @omgcheckplease · Wednesday, March 15, 2017 | 7:55 AM

@lemonitswed - i track everyone's stats. He's my boyfriend. You wish you had SO Stats, Birkholtz. =)

Eric Bittle @omgcheckplease · Friday, March 3, 2017 | 7:58 AM

He's baking while supervised. =) He's nearly done!

Eric Bittle @omgcheckplease · Tuesday, March 28, 2017 | 9:20 PM

Samwell makes the FROZEN FOUR!

Eric Bittle @omgcheckplease · Monday, April 3, 2017 | 11:21 PM

OKAY!!!! Y'ALL!!! I'm FREE. I've finished my draft and even revised it and am a step away from turning in EVERYTHING.

Eric Bittle @omgcheckplease · Monday, April 3, 2017 | 11:23 PM

And I wanted to share the news...I was asked to give THE Senior Closing Speech at Class Day!! Graduation speech!!!

Eric Bittle @omgcheckplease · Monday, April 3, 2017 | 11:29 PM

Lord in Heaven, I have so so so many things to say about this place. I just hope I don't CRY.

Eric Bittle @omgcheckplease · Saturday, April 15, 2017 | 12:03 AM

THE SAMWELL MEN'S HOCKEY TEAM IS THE NCAA NATIONAL GODDAMN CHAMPS!!!

Eric Bittle @omgcheckplease · Saturday, April 15, 2017 | 12:06 AM

WE ARE OUT AND WE ARE YELLING ON THE BUS. AND I'M OVER 21 I CAN DRINK LEGALLY.

Eric Bittle @omgcheckplease · Saturday, April 15, 2017 | 12:07 AM

AND I MAY HAVE LOST A TOOTH.

Eric Bittle @omgcheckplease · Sunday, April 23, 2017 | 4:15 PM

There's something about Dibs. The Haus. Kissing the ice. And all of the traditions we have in SMH. If I had known how much they would affect me...

Eric Bittle @omgcheckplease · Sunday, April 23, 2017 | 4:15 PM

I just love this team. this school. this Haus. my time here. I'm 100% revising my Class Day speech and getting misty eyed. Samwell.

Eric Bittle @omgcheckplease · Thursday, April 27, 2017 | 6:45 AM

So big, big, SECRET news, y'all!......I've decided to make a public twitter account while keeping this one locked. Because?

Eric Bittle @omgcheckplease · Thursday, April 27, 2017 | 6:47 AM

I MAY HAVE A BOOK DEAL IN THE WORKS!!! After graduation!! A COOKBOOK. That ties in to my vlog???? I MIGHT ACTUALLY HAVE A JOB!!!!! I'm getting an AGENT???

Eric Bittle @omgcheckplease · Friday, May 19, 2017 | 9:46 AM

Mama and Coach are officially in Samwell for Class Day, Graduation, and for meeting BOB AND ALICIA.

Eric Bittle @omgcheckplease · Friday, May 19, 2017 | 9:47 AM

So so so sorry if I'm not around. I'm running all over this campus like a chicken with my head cut off. My thesis was approved by the by!

Eric Bittle @omgcheckplease · Sunday, May 21, 2017 | 8:23 AM

For posterity: At MY graduation, Jack seems even more nervous for me than I am? Honestly, so sweet....I mean, my speech was yesterday? Very odd.

Eric Bittle @omgcheckplease · Sunday, May 21, 2017 | 8:27 AM

The Zimmermanns weren't able to make it to Class Day, but they made it down to Samwell for commencement! Bob and Alicia are such dolls! My mama is SO nervous.

Eric Bittle @omgcheckplease · Sunday, May 21, 2017 | 10:04 AM

Yes, my name is Eric Bittle and I am tweeting while waiting in line for commencement because I'm a fool overwhelmed by emotion.

Eric Bittle @omgcheckplease · Sunday, May 21, 2017 | 10:05 AM

I love this place. I love Samwell. I love my friends. I love my team. I love this place. I loved this place. I love this place. I'm still a Samwell student for another hour.

Eric Bittle @omgcheckplease · Sunday, May 21, 2017 | 10:06 AM
Four years passed by so quickly. And I grew so much. I said it in my speech yesterday. I am who I am because of this place. And y'all, I'm crying.

Eric Bittle @omgcheckplease · Sunday, May 21, 2017 | 10:08 AM
It's hard to type because I learned to love myself because of the love of my teammates and boyfriend and professors and friends and parents and family.

Eric Bittle @omgcheckplease · Sunday, May 21, 2017 | 10:09 AM
I learned to stop being afraid because of my time here and the love I felt here. I am who I am because of this. I'm so thankful. Thank you all.

Eric Bittle @omgcheckplease · Sunday, May 21, 2017 | 12:48 PM
Diploma in hand. Samwell Alum!! :-)

Eric Bittle @omgcheckplease · Sunday, May 21, 2017 | 1:35 PM
On our way to lunch and my life has changed forever.

Eric Bittle @omgcheckplease · Sunday, May 21, 2017 | 2:30 PM
I realize I just became a college graduate but MORE IMPORTANTLY
Jack: Mom, have you seen Shitty?
Alicia: Oh Byron? He found his old philosophy professor
Jack: Wait what?
Holster: wait
Ransom: wha
Lardo: The S stands for Sterling if you're wondering about that too

Eric Bittle @omgcheckplease · Sunday, May 21, 2017 | 2:31 PM
BYRON STERLING "SHITTY" KNIGHT. I'm going to EXPIRE.

Eric Bittle @omgcheckplease · Sunday, May 21, 2017 | 2:32 PM
Confronting Shitty at lunch and Shitty: B.S. Knight? B.S.? You guys know I'm full of shit.

Eric Bittle @omgcheckplease · Sunday, May 21, 2017 | 3:01 PM
Oh my goodness, Jack is so nostalgic. He asked the operations guy at Faber if he could skate there one last time. I'm down!

Eric Bittle @omgcheckplease · Sunday, May 21, 2017 | 3:58 PM

....I'm engaged.

 Eric Bittle @omgcheckplease · Sunday, May 21, 2017 | 4:01 PM

This boy. My fiancé.

 Eric Bittle @omgcheckplease · Sunday, May 21, 2017 | 8:17 PM

MY FIANCÉ!!!

 Eric Bittle @omgcheckplease · Wednesday, June 7, 2017 | 9:46 AM

Um. So I'm in Canada for the first time? I'm at Jack's parents' house! And it's delightful!...But I'm actually....making a summer resolution to try and use my Twitter less? And then only tweet for my public account?

 Eric Bittle @omgcheckplease · Wednesday, June 7, 2017 | 9:46 AM

BUT Answering all of your post-engagement questions: 1.) He asked me. I would've asked him but he beat me to it. 2.) He did get down on one knee

 Eric Bittle @omgcheckplease · Wednesday, June 7, 2017 | 9:48 AM

3.) He was EXTREMELY NERVOUS APPARENTLY 4.) My mom SCREAMED about it even though Jack had talked to my mom about it? And most importantly, 5) I FAINTED

 Eric Bittle @omgcheckplease · Wednesday, June 7, 2017 | 10:04 AM

But we're off! Jack is showing me his old stomping grounds, and then we'll be back in time for some dinner made by Bad Bob Zimmermann? And after that?

 Eric Bittle @omgcheckplease · Wednesday, June 7, 2017 | 12:00 PM

Well, I think I'll bake a pie. <3

First Second

Published by First Second
First Second is an imprint of Roaring Brook Press,
a division of Holtzbrinck Publishing Holdings Limited Partnership
120 Broadway, New York, NY 10271

Don't miss your next favorite book from First Second! For the latest updates go
to firstsecondnewsletter.com and sign up for our enewsletter.

Library of Congress Control Number: 2019930756

Hardcover ISBN: 978-1-250-17949-4
Paperback ISBN: 978-1-250-17950-0

Our books may be purchased in bulk for promotional, educational, or business use.
Please contact your local bookseller or the Macmillan Corporate and Premium Sales Department
at (800) 221-7945 ext. 5442 or by email at MacmillanSpecialMarkets@macmillan.com.

First edition, 2020
Edited by Calista Brill and Kiara Valdez
Book design by Molly Johanson and Chris Dickey
Printed in China

Paperback: 10 9 8 7 6 5 4 3 2 1
Hardcover: 10 9 8 7 6 5 4 3 2 1